PROJECT
DISASTER

Have you read these books?

- ❏ *Aliens in the Basement* • Suzan Reid
- ❏ *The Big Race!* • Sylvia McNicoll
- ❏ *A Ghost in the Attic* • Suzan Reid
- ❏ *Howard's House is Haunted* • Maureen Bayless
- ❏ *Liar, Liar, Pants on Fire* • Gordon Korman
- ❏ *The Lost Locket* • Carol Matas
- ❏ *Monsters in the School* • Martyn Godfrey
- ❏ *Princesses Don't Wear Jeans* • Brenda Bellingham
- ❏ *Project Disaster* • Sylvia McNicoll
- ❏ *School Campout* • Becky Citra
- ❏ *Sleepover Zoo* • Brenda Kearns
- ❏ *Starring Me!* • Cathy Miyata
- ❏ *Wonder Dog* • Beverly Scudamore
- ❏ *Worm Pie* • Beverly Scudamore

PROJECT DISASTER

Sylvia McNicoll

Cover by
Greg Banning

Interior illustrations by
Brian Boyd

Scholastic Canada Ltd.

Special thanks to Mrs. Cowles' Grade Two class at Clarksdale School for their input.

Canadian Cataloguing in Publication Data

McNicoll, Sylvia, 1954-
Project disaster

(Shooting Star)
ISBN 0-590-73742-2

I. Boyd, Brian. II. Title. III. Series.

PS8575.N53P76 1990   jC813'.54   C90-094891-4
PZ7.M265Pr 1990

10 9 8 7 6 5   **Printed in Canada**   0 1 2 3 4/0

Contents

To Mom and Dad —
my children's Omi and Opa

Chapter 1

Breaking Training

"**A**nd now Fido, the amazing trained goldfish, will leap out of the water and take fish food from my hand." I was pretending we were in front of the class presenting my project.

I'd been practising with Fido for weeks, feeding him at exactly the same time every day, calling his name, holding the food higher and higher, waiting until he swam to the top of the water to finally let him have a food flake.

Today was the day.

"Jump, Fido, jump!"

Fido swam up quickly. Project Pet was looking good. Then he stopped near the surface.

"Come on, boy. You can do it."

Fido didn't think so. He swished his tail back and forth, his head shook, and he opened and closed his mouth.

"No, no, no," it looked like he was saying.

"O.K., I'll hold the food lower so it's not so hard," I promised.

Swish, swish. "No, no, no," Fido mouthed again.

"What's wrong, boy? Aren't you hungry?" I asked him.

My little sister Tara came up beside me. "No, I already fed Fido fishy," she said.

"You what!" I yelled.

"Just some cracker," Tara said. "He saw me eating one and he wanted it." She picked up the fish food can and before I could stop her she started shaking more flakes in. "Now Fido can have dessert," she said.

"Don't!" I screamed. Tara ignored me and kept shaking more food into the fishbowl. I grabbed Tara's hand and shook it until she let go of the little square can.

"He's my fish, Tara. Leave him alone!" I yelled as I pushed her away. She stumbled and managed to bump into the wall — but not very hard.

Tara cried, of course. Loudly, too, like the siren on Dad's police car. "Wuaa-aaa-aaa-aaa."

Just then, Dad rushed by. He was dressed in his uniform and heading for the door. Tara's crying stopped him.

"What happened here?" Dad demanded. "Neil? Quickly, I have to be at the station in 15 minutes."

"Tara accidentally bumped her head," I explained.

"Did not. Neil pushed me. Wuaaa-aaa-aaa-aaa," Tara sobbed.

"Neil!" Dad said it as if it was my fault.

"I didn't do it on purpose, Dad. She keeps feeding Fido and I told her to stop." I explained.

"Neil, she's only four years old," Dad said. "What do you expect?"

"But Dad, she could kill him!" I said.

"Just clean out his bowl. Your silly fish will be fine," Dad said.

"He's not a silly fish. It's not his fault he's not a dog," I mumbled.

"Look, Neil, you know what I told you. Work harder in school and we'll see about the dog." Dad rubbed and kissed The Baby's head to make her stop crying. She finally did. He looked up at me. "Don't you have any homework to do?"

"All finished, Dad. It's a project on Fido. I typed it on Mom's computer and everything." It was a great report. Miss Rosonoff just had to give me an A on it. And then Dad would have to get me a dog.

"That's good, Neil," Dad said. "I'm counting on you to help us out this week. While your mom's in the hospital, I want you to be on your best behaviour."

"Sure, Dad," I answered, even though I didn't feel like being good just then.

"No more fighting now," he called out just

before he left. "Bye."

I waited until he'd driven away. Then I gave Tara a little shove and ran outside before anyone could get me for it.

My grandfather was outside polishing his car. I slammed the door behind me but he didn't even seem to notice. He just kept polishing the Firebird.

He loves that car, and so do I.

My grandparents don't usually live with us. They were visiting because Mom was in the hospital having another baby. I thought Tara was plenty, but nobody had asked me.

Anyway, they were taking care of Tara for Mom. I didn't mind—I think they're great. And so's the Firebird. It's the neatest machine on the road and it's a lucky car too because my grandfather won it in a contest.

I moved closer to the Firebird. It was black and shiny. I breathed in the smell of the wax my grandfather was using on it. It smelled like a combination of wood and soap. An exciting smell.

"Can I help, Opa?" (Opa means grandpa in German.) I leaned over and ran my hand over the Firebird. It felt smooth, and it was hot from the sun.

Opa stopped whistling and looked over at me. "Careful, careful, don't lean on the car. Your zipper might scratch the finish." He smiled.

I quickly stepped back.

"Here," Opa tossed me a rag, "you do the wheels."

"O.K.," I said and knelt down to work. I pushed a corner of the rag around a spoke and then gently moved the rag up and down.

"Hi, Neil. This must be your grandfather's car. Decent!" My best friend Marc Guilbert had just walked up.

"Hi, Marc. Yeah, this is it." I stood up, folded my arms and leaned back against the fender. Opa looked over and I quickly stepped away again. Opa nodded and smiled at Marc.

"Do you think we could go for a ride?" Marc asked.

I looked over at Opa.

"When Neil's finished with the wheel," he promised.

"Finished," I called out. I threw the rag down into Opa's bin.

"All right. I'll just go in and wash up," Opa said.

Meanwhile Marc and I flung open the doors and hopped in.

I sank down in the smooth black seat behind the steering wheel. I felt like the pilot sliding into the cockpit of a jet fighter. Marc was my co-pilot.

"Whoa, is this ever excellent. Wonder what it feels like to drive. Do you think it's hard?" asked Marc.

"Nah. I could drive it," I said.

"Come on. You could not," Marc said.

"Sure I could. Last week — when Dad and I were fooling around with the go-karts at the mall — I never knocked one pylon down. Dad said I was a great driver," I bragged.

"Yeah, right, like you would ever drive your

grandfather's Firebird," Marc replied.

"I might, if I was in the right mood," I defended myself.

"Aw no, look! Your grandfather's bringing Tara," cried Marc.

"Great. I can't ever do anything without The Baby around," I grumbled.

"Doesn't she need a special seat or something?" Marc said.

"No, but you get to sit in the back with her. Out of my seat now," I said, pointing.

Marc climbed in the back then and I shifted over to the co-pilot's side. Tara got in beside Marc.

Opa opened the T-roof and then started the engine. VRROOOOM. I love that noise.

"Seatbelts on everyone?" Opa asked.

"Yeah," Marc answered.

"We're off!" Opa shouted above the noise. The tires screeched as we backed out of the driveway and blasted off. I saw my grandmother shaking her head in the window. I waved to her.

"All right!" Marc shouted.

Opa took us out on the Trans-Canada Highway then and really made the Firebird fly. After a few minutes he glanced at the speedometer. The Firebird slowed down slightly.

"Your Dad wouldn't be on radar patrol here, would he?" Opa asked.

"No, not on the highway," I answered.

The first time Opa and I had gone cruising, he hadn't paid enough attention to how fast he was going and Dad had stopped him in a speed trap. I don't think Dad realized it was us.

Boy, was Dad mad, even madder when he noticed I was in the car. He even gave Opa a ticket. Dad's seen a lot of crashes because of his job, and he hates speeders.

"Wish someone from school could see us," Marc said.

"Yeah, me too," I agreed.

"Wheeeeeeeeee," Tara called out.

"Can we drive around to my house so my mom can see?" Marc asked.

Opa nodded. We got off the highway and

doubled back.

"Could you just honk the horn?" Marc asked as we drove up.

Mrs. Guilbert waved from the window and ran out. "I hear your mother's had the baby, Neil. Was it a girl or a boy?"

She didn't even notice the car.

"A boy," I said.

"How nice! A brother for you! Why don't you all stop in and have some cookies."

"Thank you. I need to run an errand," Opa said. "Neil, do you want to stay for a while?"

"Me too. Me too, Opa?" Tara begged.

"No, you have to let the boys play by themselves," Opa answered.

Tara opened her mouth to cry but Mrs. Guilbert was faster. "The boys don't mind, do you Marc?"

"You can't stay, Tara," I said.

"Sure she can," Marc said in a strange voice. What was with him? He winked at me. "Let her stay. I've got something to show Tara."

Chapter 2

Don't Pat the Snake!

Mrs. Guilbert's cookies tasted awful, not like Mom's at all. Who ever heard of putting coconut in chocolate chip cookies? Tara didn't mind, though. I thought she'd never stop eating.

"Let's go, Neil. I'll show you my traders," Marc said. "You coming?" he said to Tara.

She shoved a fourth cookie in her mouth and followed us to Marc's room.

Marc handed me a stack of hockey cards. "They're mostly Toronto Maple Leafs. I'd trade all of them for one Wayne Gretzky."

Both Marc and I collect the hockey cards that come in Superstar Cereal. I hate Superstars but Claude, Dad's partner, eats through boxes of it and saves the cards for me, so I had a great collection anyway.

"I don't have Wayne Gretzky yet. But I'll look them over and see what I want to trade," I said.

"What are you going to show me?" Tara asked.

"Yeah, what are you going to show her?" I repeated. Then I noticed that Marc was reaching into an aquarium with sand, a couple of rocks, a dish of water and . . .

His snake, of course! Marc pulled out his hand and he was holding what looked like a thin striped garden hose except that it twisted and coiled around his arm.

Tara's mouth dropped open.

"Tara, meet Slinky. He's my Project Pet for school," Marc said. He lowered his arm to Tara's shoulder.

No, Marc, don't! I thought, but I didn't say it out loud. We both wanted to teach Tara a lesson, didn't we? We didn't want her to always hang around us and spoil our fun.

I saw Marc's sneaky smile spread across his face. The snake slithered down Tara's arm.

Tara started giggling. "It tickles. Hee, hee, hee, hee." Tara grabbed the snake and patted it.

I should have known. Tara thinks garden slugs are cute! Boy, the one time you expect The Baby to scream and cry, she laughs. Now we'd wrecked our morning for nothing.

"Here. Give him back. You're not supposed to pat snakes!" Marc said to Tara.

"Why not? Can I feed Slinky?" Tara begged.

"No, you can't!" Marc snapped.

"Come on, Tara. We'd better go home. It's almost time for lunch," I added.

"Yeah, I'll see you later," Marc said to me. His back was toward me and he didn't look around. He lowered Slinky back into the aquarium. "Without The Baby," he added.

"Yeah," I agreed. I took off out the door.

I walked really fast on the way home. Tara was almost running to keep up but she didn't cry or complain. Of course not — no one was there to hear.

The moment Tara got home, she headed for the fishbowl again.

"Why is Fido swimming so funny?" Tara asked.

"What do you mean, swimming funny?" I asked. I hurried over to check it out. Fido was trying his best to swim upright but every couple of fin flicks, he flopped over on his side and floated for a while.

"Oh no, Fido's sick!" I grabbed the fish bowl and moved it back and forth. That helped, but only for about ten fin flicks, then he drifted back near the surface again.

Fido struggled to swim. His black dot eyes stared into mine and his mouth opened and closed. "Please, please, please," he seemed to say to me.

"Just keep moving, Fido!"

Fido waved his fins a couple of times and then floated up again.

"You see what you've done, Tara. Feeding

him crackers, now look!" I was so mad I kicked the table. Dirty water splashed over the top of the bowl. Fido swam again, maybe out of surprise.

That gave me an idea.

I ran up the stairs with the bowl. I filled the bathroom sink with fresh water and dumped Fido in. When he still flopped over, I pushed him a bit with my green fish net.

"I want to try. Let me try," Tara whined from behind me.

"Get lost, Tara. This is all your fault." I shoved her out of the bathroom and slammed the door.

Tara howled. "Neil pushed me!" she cried.

"Nee–il," my grandmother called up from the kitchen, "can't you be nice to your sister?"

Why does everyone always jump to her side? I thought. There was nothing more I could do for Fido so I stepped out of the bathroom too and shut the door again.

"Aw, stop your crying! I didn't touch you," I said.

Tara just got louder.

She was now sobbing so hard her shoulders were shaking and the little red duck barrettes in her blond hair were bobbing up and down.

"Stop crying and I'll play cards with you," I said. That's how desperate I was. I was sure she couldn't hear me above her crying.

But she did.

"O.K." She straightened up fast, gave her eyes a rub and sniffed a few times.

"Fine. Come into my, er, our room." *My* room had become *our* room as soon as Mom had told us she was going to have a new baby.

Tara followed me like a puppy as usual. It was too bad she wasn't a dog, I thought. She'd be more fun.

I gave her Marc's traders and I took another stack of my own hockey cards from my desk. I told her how the game worked. The closest card to the wall won, a card landing on top of another won the bottom card. Then I showed her how to throw, with the corner of the card between two fingers and her hand bent around almost like a boomerang. I had to put the card between her fingers and bend her hand and arm.

The card flopped in the air like a sick bird.

I showed her again and held her hand as she threw so that a few cards at least went in the right direction. Then I let her try by herself again.

The card hit me in the eye.

"Ow! Not like that, Tara." Sigh. "You practise a while by yourself, O.K.?" I showed her again. Then I took the pillow off my bed and lay back on the floor with it.

FWUMP, FWUMP, FWUMP, the cards would go if Tara hit anything at all.

I stared at the ceiling. There were fluorescent stickers up there — little yellow flecks that turned into the moon, the stars and Halley's comet when the room got dark. Dad had put them up for me years ago, before Tara was even born.

I loved my stars.

Only Tara hated sleeping in the dark. With the door open and hall light on, I could never see the galaxy glowing any more. When the new baby grew up a bit and didn't sleep in a crib, I'd probably have to share my room with him instead. I hoped he wouldn't mind the dark.

FWUMP, FWUMP, FWUMP. Tara was getting better aim. I heard someone coming up the stairs.

FWUMP, FWUMP, FWOOOOOOSH.

That last noise was the toilet flushing. I didn't think of Fido until I heard the sound of water running. Then it hit me — my grandmother must be washing her hands over Fido.

"Omi, Omi!" I called out and ran to the bathroom.

I heard her shocked voice over the rushing water. "Meine Güte," she shouted.

Chapter 3

There's a Shark in the Sink

"**O**mi" means grandma in German and "Meine Güte!" just means "My Goodness!" It isn't swearing or anything, but it's as close as my grandmother gets. She was standing in the bathroom rubbing her hands. She had a pained expression on her face, as if she'd touched something disgusting.

"Is that your goldfish, Neil?" she asked.

"Uh, yeah." I looked at Fido. The sudden gush of water had helped him to swim a few healthy-looking laps around the sink.

Was he cured? I wondered.

No. He slowed down, drifted onto his side and began floating to the top again.

"It's O.K., isn't it Omi? He's sick and I think swimming in the sink gives him more oxygen," I explained.

She looked like she wanted to say no.

"Please Omi. I have to try to make him better," I begged.

"All right. But only until tonight," she finally said. "Where is Tara now?"

"In my room, playing cards." I stopped to listen.

SHWIZZT, SHWIZZT, SHWIZZT. That wasn't the noise the cards made hitting the wall. We both walked to the room and peeked in.

SHWIZZT, SHWIZZT, SHWIZZT. That was the noise the hockey cards made as Tara ripped them into pieces.

"Oh no!" I rushed over to her and shook a card loose from her fist. "Look at what you've done!" I hollered.

That started her police car siren again.

"Wuaa-aaa-aaa-aaa."

"Tara, you know better than to rip your brother's cards," Omi said.

Tara cried louder.

"I think someone needs to take a nap," Omi told her. Then she looked at me. "Neil, would you play downstairs?" she said.

I grabbed the cards and stomped down the stairs as loudly as I could.

I went to the kitchen to tape the cards back together. Tara had torn up eight of Marc's Toronto Maple Leaf traders.

I tried to line the pieces up right but it was impossible. Now I'd owe Marc a Wayne Gretzky card no matter what.

So for fun I matched up the wrong bodies to the wrong heads. The cards were wrecked anyway. Marc wouldn't take them back like that. I pencilled in mustaches, beards, earrings and eye patches. The Toronto Maple Leafs never looked better.

Omi finally came down the stairs. "Tara's resting now. She's just overtired."

"Do you want to play 'Pizza Party' with me?" I asked her.

"No, no. I'm sorry, Neil. When Opa comes home from the store with the Ivory Snow, I have to wash all the baby sheets and clothes." Omi smiled and then hugged me.

I pulled away. The new baby wasn't even home yet and he already got more attention than I did.

"Just think, another baby in the house," Omi said as if it was something wonderful. "Won't it be nice to have a new baby brother?"

"No," I mumbled. It would have been nice to have an older big brother, not another baby to follow me around.

Opa came home from the store then. "Hi Neil. Here you go, Monika." He put the bag on the counter and kissed Omi's cheek.

I noticed a bag of my favourite green jujubes sticking out of his back pocket. Without turning around, Opa reached into his pocket and flipped the bag to me. When he turned around, he winked.

24

"I think I'll go watch television," I said to Omi so that I could sneak off to the basement and eat my jujubes before lunch.

"O.K.," Omi said.

I went downstairs to our TV room. Now where had Tara put the remote control? I gave up looking for it and pushed the ON button on the set. "Sesame Street," Tara's favourite show. I switched over to "Teenage Mutant Ninja Turtles" and ate about five jujubes before Opa came tearing down the stairs.

"Neil, Neil, there's a shark swimming in the sink," he said. He was out of breath from running.

"Come on, Opa," I said. He's such a joker.

"You're right, he's not swimming," Opa said.

"Aw no! He's not dead, is he Opa?" I cried.

Opa just put his hand on my shoulder.

Chapter 4

Burial at Sea

Fido was floating on his side in the sink. He stared up at me with one dead black eye. I had to look away. I didn't want to cry over a fish.

"You don't want to flush him down the toilet, do you?" Opa asked me.

I shook my head.

"Why don't we go down to the river and throw him in. Don't you think he would like that better?" Opa suggested.

"Yeah — like a burial at sea." I felt a bit better.

Opa got an empty mayonnaise jar and scooped Fido from the sink. "Let's go," he said.

"We're going to Fairview Shopping Centre," Opa told Omi, "after the funeral, that is. Do you need anything?"

"No. But we were all supposed to go to the hospital with Jean-Pierre at three." (Jean-Pierre's my Dad).

"We will meet you there," Opa answered.

"Auf Wiedersehen!" Omi said to us as we left. (That's pronounced *owf vee-duh-zayn*, and it means "until we meet again," in German.) We walked outside to the car.

I felt better as soon as I sat in the Firebird. Big and important.

VROOOOOOOOOM. And then the screech of the tires. I loved it.

"Opa, do you think I could drive a car?" I asked.

"Oh sure, any idiot can drive. Just look around you," he answered.

I wasn't sure what he meant but I started watching him closely. It looked like it was mostly just steering.

Opa parked the car along the side of the road

near the river and we walked down to the river bank. There were trees hanging over the green water.

Yeah, Fido would have liked this.

I held the jar for a while staring at him. I'd never realized before then what a beautiful colour he was. It was hard to just throw him away like a broken toy.

"I really liked Fido," I said to Opa. "He wasn't a dog, but he was the best fish . . . I had him trained to swim to the top of the water when I called him and I was trying to get him to jump out of the water to take food from my hand."

"Did he?" Opa asked.

"No. Maybe if Tara hadn't fed him on the sly and if I'd had another few days." I swallowed hard then. "His favourite colour was green — just like mine."

"How did you know that?"

"I took out a book on goldfish from the library, you know, for Project Pet."

"This book told you that Fido's favourite colour was green?" Opa asked.

"No. It said that if you put different colours of construction paper under the bowl, the fish would swim toward its favourite colour. Fido liked green. I was going to show the class."

"Come, Neil," Opa said, and he put his arm around my shoulder.

"In a second," I said. It was no use. Fido was stiff and dead now. I took a breath and poured my only pet from the jar into the river.

"Auf Wiedersehen, Fido. We'll see you in the next world again," Opa shouted out and waved.

For a moment Fido floated on the water. Then the river washed him away.

"Goodbye," I whispered softly.

Chapter 5

The Firebird is Mine

I knew what Opa had in mind the moment we walked into Fairview Shopping Centre, but he didn't rush me into it. First we ate double scoop ice cream waffle cones for lunch and then we looked around in a toy store for a while.

"Why don't we buy your baby brother a present from you?" Opa suggested. "You know the best kind of present to give is one you enjoy yourself. Is there some special toy you would like that maybe you can show him how to use?"

I picked up a mechanical construction kit, but Opa read on the box that it was not for children under three years old. I looked around again.

"How about these? They're for babies!" I showed Opa a container of giant-size plastic Mega Blocks. I'd always wanted some but I was too big for them.

Opa agreed, and he paid for them on our way out.

"Let's go to the book store," Opa suggested then. "I would like to buy your mother a book."

I like book stores too, so I agreed.

We split up in the store. Opa wandered around in the front adult section while I checked out the kids' books at the back.

Opa joined me after about 15 minutes. He had a big thick book under his arm — probably the life story of someone famous. Mom loves those.

"Pick something for yourself and Tara," Opa said.

They had great dinosaur picture books with little windows that I was dying to open, so I picked one for Tara. For me, it was a lot harder. I'd read all the "Choose-your-own-adventure" books they had. Maybe I'd get a mystery.

"Oh look!" Opa pointed. "They have *Charlotte's Web* in paperback now. Your mother used to love that book."

I chose *Charlotte's Web*. I guess I wondered what Mom had liked when she was a kid.

Opa paid for the books.

Finally, we went to the pet shop. So I was right about why we were at the mall. We walked down the aisles pretending we didn't know exactly why we were there.

We looked at the gerbils and hamsters, birds and kittens and I spent a lot of time at the window where the puppies were.

Opa moved away first. He dragged me over to the aquariums, but once I was there I stopped. I couldn't look at another fish.

"But Neil, what are you going to do for your project?" Opa asked.

Project Pet — I'd forgotten all about it.

"Aw, Opa, I could never train another fish in just six days," I said, but it wasn't only that. How could I just buy a different fish and put him in Fido's bowl and feed him Fido's food? It wouldn't feel right.

"O.K." Opa never tried to talk me into things. "I need to buy some film," he said as we walked out, so we went into a camera store.

On the wall of the shop there was a poster of a beautiful RV, like a big trailer home except with captain's seats and a steering wheel. MOTORING WITH MINOLTA the poster read and there was a pad of entry forms for a contest to win the RV in the picture.

"Isn't that a decent machine?" Opa said. He sounded like he was making fun of Marc. "Here," he handed me his red container of name and address labels. "Stick these on a few of the entries while I get the film."

I did better than that. I took the whole pad. That way no one else could enter.

I licked and stuck, licked and stuck, licked and stuck until my tongue got tired. Then I had to fill in Opa's phone number. Luckily Opa took a long time buying the film. I took an even longer time filling out the entry forms.

"Neil, Neil. Hurry up, it's a quarter after

three. Children's visiting hours are at 3:30," Opa said.

He didn't know that I had filled up the whole pad. I gave him back his address labels.

"Opa, what would you do if you won the RV?" I asked.

"Well, I'd drive it down to Disney World and take a few grandchildren with me." Opa winked.

Yeah, that sounded good. "But what about the Firebird?" I wanted to know.

Opa didn't even have to think about it. "The Firebird would be yours."

Chapter 6

I Meet Jello-Neck

The Firebird would be mine. I thought about that all the way to the hospital. With his luck, and with all the entry forms I'd filled out, Opa was sure to win the RV.

And then the Firebird *was* mine.

By the time we found a parking spot, bought some flowers for Mom, and caught the elevator up to the maternity ward, there was only 15 minutes of visiting time left for kids.

Dad was in the corner of Mom's room. I could see him as we walked down the hall. He had a blue hospital gown on and his uniform shirt was rolled up at the sleeves. He held a tiny bundle in his big hands.

The bundle could have been laundry except for the way Dad was looking at it.

Dad was smiling. There were a million tiny wrinkles around his mouth and eyes. His eyes were shiny as if he was going to cry and they were looking straight into the baby's eyes.

Dad never looks at me like that. He usually eyeballs me the way he does a car that's parked in a tow-away zone.

Opa and I breezed into the room.

"Enfin!" Dad said. (That means "at last" in French. Dad only says stuff in French when he's annoyed.)

Opa just shrugged his shoulders. "Hello Jean-Pierre," he said. "Neil and I were having such fun we lost track of time." Then he strode over to Mom and kissed her cheek. "You look wonderful," he said to her. "How are you?"

"Tired but fine," Mom said. "Hi Neil, are those for me?" She smiled as I handed her the flowers.

"Yeah," I answered as I hugged Mom.

"Aren't they lovely?" Omi said and after a few seconds she took the flowers from Mom's hand. "I'll get a vase and some water for them."

"Uh, these are for him," I said to Dad, handing him the toy store bag.

"Well now, what did your big brother get you?" Dad shifted the bundle of laundry to one arm and took the bag. Then he slid the box of brightly coloured blocks onto his knee.

Tara scrambled over. "I want to open them. Can I? Can I?"

Dad held them out of her reach. "No, Tara. We don't want to lose any. They're for the baby."

"Why didn't I get anything?" Tara whined.

"Quiet, dummy!" I said to her. "We'll get to play with them, too."

But she started to cry anyway.

Just as she was getting ready to do her police car siren, Opa jingled some change in his pocket. "Tara, did I see some vending machines at the end of the hall?"

"Yes," she said and ran off to show him.

"Thank you," Mom said. Opa just winked and left the room.

Dad lowered the Mega Blocks and waved them in front of the bundle. Then he put the blocks down.

"Thank you, Neil," Mom said. "I'm sure your little brother will love playing with those blocks."

"Neil, if you wash your hands really well in the sink over there," my father pointed to the bathroom, "I have an extra hospital gown here for you so you can hold your brother."

I wasn't sure I wanted to, but I scrubbed my hands and put the hospital gown on anyway.

"He's so light!" I couldn't help saying as I took him from Dad.

"His head! Hold his head," Dad said as he let go.

Geez. The little guy's head was attached with Jello instead of a neck. I put my hand underneath his head. He scrunched up his face the way Tara just had and then changed his mind in mid-scrunch. He opened his eyes and looked like he'd just noticed a butterfly at the end of my nose.

"Oh no, he's cross-eyed," I said.

"No, no, Neil. Most babies' eyes go that way till they're stronger," Dad explained.

"Good," I said. Imagine having a little cross-eyed brother to explain to Marc.

I patted the soft black down on his head and felt his pulse bumping in and out at the top of his head.

Just like that I found myself kissing his small warm cheek. There was hardly enough room for my lips.

I liked his hands the best. His tiny fingers were bunched up into a fist — maybe he'd grow up to be a boxer. I touched his perfect little fingernails as softly as I could. It scared him though, because he threw out his skinny arms in a karate chop.

"Easy, Neil," Dad warned and took my brother back.

"Can you think of a good name?" Dad asked

me. "Maybe Jean-Pierre like his dad," he said softly, and he looked at the baby again in that strange, goofy way.

"No," I answered. Why didn't they name me Jean-Pierre?

The nurse came in with a glass crib on wheels, sort of like a fish tank for babies. She took my brother from Dad and put him in the crib.

She wheeled away what had to be the ugliest, most wrinkled-up baby I'd ever seen. I liked him for that.

But I hated that Dad liked him so much. I hated that Dad liked Tara better than me, too, but at least she's sort of cute with her duck barrettes and all.

"Omi tells me Fido died," Mom said. "Did Opa buy you another goldfish at the mall?"

"No. I wouldn't let him."

"But what about Project Pet? Can you read your report without a pet?" Mom asked.

"I don't care," I said.

"Neil, you have to care," Dad said. "Remember our deal. If you don't do better, no dog."

"Too bad you couldn't bring your sister," Omi said as Tara skipped back into the room chewing something. "Or your little brother. They're both such pets."

Too bad I couldn't drive the Firebird right into the classroom. Now that's a pet the kids would be interested in.

I tried to picture driving the Firebird through the front door of the school. All the bricks would crumble around the sides as I plowed through. Yes, I could see it and I loved it.

Then Dad was shaking my shoulder. "Neil, time to go. Your mother needs to rest."

Chapter 7

Project Pet

The good thing about Tara sharing my room was that with the door open and the hall light on, I could read late even on school nights.

The bad thing was that when she cried for Mom, I was the one who had to listen to her.

It was Wednesday night, and Tara was crying for Mom for the fourth night in a row.

"Stop it, Tara. Come into my bed and I'll read you your book," I said. I felt a little bit sorry for her because I was lonely for Mom too.

We looked at all the windows in her new dinosaur book together. Then I read to her from

Charlotte's Web. Finally she fell asleep.

I read on.

Charlotte's Web is about this pig, Wilbur, who was raised as a little girl's pet. What a great Project Pet he'd have made!

My eyes felt tired so I grabbed a hockey card off my desk and stuck it in as a bookmark. I lay back down and closed my eyes. A pig, a pig, a pig — I imagined walking Wilbur into the classroom on a leash. Then I got him to sit on Miss Rosonoff's desk as I read my report. Everyone loved him — they all clapped and crowded around me. Usually everyone just yawns.

Wilbur took a bow on the desk. He even smiled.

Suddenly it was as if it was really happening. I guess I was dreaming. I walked around letting all the kids pat Wilbur, telling them things about him, answering questions like "Where does he sleep?"

Where did he sleep? Right in my arms in my own bed. You know the strange way dreams jump you around to different places — well, suddenly I was in my bed sleeping with Wilbur. I felt his pink skin and it was much softer than you'd expect — like a baby's. His breath was hot against my shoulder even through my pyjamas. It seemed so real.

Then it was morning, Thursday morning. Tara was in my arms when I woke up. It was her breath that I'd felt.

One more day to go before I had to show my Project Pet.

At school Mario brought in his turtle, Zippy. We all crowded round to watch Zippy lounge under a plastic palm tree. Mario sprinkled some freeze-dried flies in the water and finally his turtle showed some zip. I'd never seen little turtle legs move so fast.

Everyone clapped.

Next, it was Ryan's turn. He brought Cadbury, his pet rabbit, to the front of the class on a leash. That took a while. On the way he explained how Cadbury was kitty litter trained so that he didn't need to be caged.

But Ryan didn't bring any kitty litter with him

and Cadbury confused the grey tile for his litter box.

The class giggled.

They would have really liked Fido feeding from my hand.

The last pet was Lindsay's parrot, Lucky. She sat his huge cage on Miss Rosonoff's desk.

Then she tried to get him to talk. "Hello, how are you Lucky?"

Lucky swayed from side to side on the wooden bar he was perched on.

"Hello, how are you Lucky?" Lindsay repeated.

Lucky walked, claw over claw, up the side of the cage across the top and back down to his bar. He seemed a little nervous.

"Hello, hello, hello," Lindsay said, as if she was testing a broken microphone.

Back up and over the cage Lucky paced.

Lindsay sighed. She went ahead with the rest of her report telling us how long parrots live and what they eat, the dull stuff. Then she put the cover back over Lucky's cage.

Lucky squawked. He didn't like the dark.

Then he croaked out, "Clean up this mess. Clean up this mess. You're not going anywhere till you clean up this mess."

Well, that even beat Cadbury's "accident."

Lindsay turned red and Miss Rosonoff laughed so hard she needed a Kleenex after.

When everyone had settled down again and Miss Rosonoff had finished wiping the tears away, she ticked off the names of the kids bringing pets the next day. Robin was bringing her dog, Marc his snake and I was bringing . . . what was I bringing now?

"Neil Boisvert, are you listening?" Miss Rosonoff called.

"Uh, yes, Miss Rosonoff," I answered, stalling for time. I wasn't going to tell them I didn't have a pet. I couldn't.

"You're still bringing your trained goldfish tomorrow?" she asked.

"Yes, I mean no. I have a new Project Pet that I want to show the class." Now why did I go and say that?

"Would you like to tell us what it is?" Miss Rosonoff asked.

"No. It'll be a surprise," I answered. Boy, would it ever. Even to me.

"Very well. We'll look forward to that." She smiled.

I sank into my chair. I thought of the report I'd typed about Fido. It had taken me three hours. I'd worked so hard. Without Fido, it was nothing.

"Hey Neil, so what are you bringing tomorrow?" Marc asked me after school.

"It's a secret," I answered.

"Come on, come on. You can tell me," he said.

"You'll find out tomorrow, Marc."

He'd have argued more but Opa drove up in the Firebird just then. Marc didn't want to talk himself out of a ride in it.

"Where to, Marc?" Opa asked as we hopped in.

"Uh, well, did you need any of my traders, Neil?" I knew he wasn't really interested in his stack of hockey cards. He just couldn't stand waiting to find out what the new pet was.

"Yeah . . . " well, I'd picked eight out of his stack anyway, "but I've got to work out some last-minute details on my pet report. I don't have time to trade with you now."

"Mmm, pet report, I can't wait to see what you've got," Marc said.

Opa gave me a look. He pulled up into Marc's driveway and let him out. Marc jumped out and went inside, letting the screen door slam.

Opa turned to me then. "What's up, Neil? You didn't really come up with a new pet, did you?"

"No, I just couldn't admit that I had nothing to show tomorrow," I admitted.

"What do the kids without animals do?" Opa asked.

"They just give a report on a pet they'd like to have, and draw pictures," I said.

"So read Project Fido without Fido. Or write about dogs. You love dogs."

"Robin's bringing a dog. I'm rotten at drawing anyway," I said.

"Then think of another animal you'd like.

Maybe there's a picture you can cut out of one of my magazines," Opa offered.

"A pig," I said, suddenly remembering my dream.

"A pig! Why a pig?" Opa looked puzzled.

"I guess because of Wilbur, you know, the pig in *Charlotte's Web*. Wilbur the amazing pig."

"It seems to me you've missed the whole point of the book," said Opa. I frowned at him. "Wilbur isn't the most amazing creature in that book, really." Opa's eyes sparkled.

By this time the Firebird was rolling into our driveway.

"Think about it," Opa said. He tossed me the keys. "Would you hang those up in the garage for me, please?"

I took the keys and hung them on the pegboard lining the wall. Then I saw something moving in the corner and Opa's idea finally made sense to me. It was big and black and ugly. And I could use Fido's old fishbowl, too.

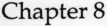

Chapter 8

Project Disaster

Robin's dog Prince had to be the neatest pet brought to class so far. He didn't look royal. He was just a brown mutt with a wagging tail and a friendly tongue that licked everybody as he padded up to the front of the class.

Everyone knew what dogs ate and that they slept at night and needed walks, so Robin concentrated on making Prince do tricks. She wanted him to shake hands. Instead he just licked her fingers and grinned as if he was embarrassed for her. Then he lay down and rolled over, thumping his tail and begging with his eyes for someone to rub his tummy.

"Awwww! He's so cute," the girls in the front said. Jenny Sommers ran over and patted his tummy.

Then it was Marc's turn. He likes dogs just as much as I do, but his mom has allergies.

"Snakes are quite beautiful when you look at them closely," Marc began as he lifted Slinky out.

"Ew, yuck! Gross!" some kids called out.

Marc grinned. "See the beautiful stripes on my pet Slinky?"

He held the snake really close to Jenny. She backed right up against her chair.

"Slinky is a garter snake. He likes eating live insects . . . "

"Ew," someone called out again.

"And he sheds his skin as he grows." As Marc talked, he moved closer to Miss Rosonoff. She was sitting at her desk. "A lot of people think snakes are slimy — but that's not true, is it Miss Rosonoff?"

Marc suddenly dropped Slinky right in front

of Miss Rosonoff. The whole class waited to see what would happen. Nobody breathed.

Miss Rosonoff stayed put for a few moments with her mouth tight and Slinky slithering towards her.

She did not want to pat or feed Slinky the way Tara had, I could tell. I think she liked Slinky about as much as I did — not at all.

Then slowly she scraped her chair back and stood up. Marc was still grinning. Miss Rosonoff picked Slinky up. She blinked hard. Then she handed him back to Marc.

Miss Rosonoff cleared her throat then. "No, Marc, you're right. He feels dry and . . . leathery," she said.

Marc blushed. Miss Rosonoff started wiping off the board very slowly and calmly. Then she put some notes about Slinky on the board.

"Thank you, Marc," she said at the end of his talk. "Neil?" she called.

I got up and walked to the front with Fido's old bowl. I knew my new report would be the best yet.

"My pet Charlotte has two jaws, eight eyes and eight legs," I began.

This report wasn't typed. But I'd written it out in my very best handwriting. Opa had taken me to the library the night before and I had found out a lot of decent things about my new pet.

"She has poison glands in her two jaws and when she sinks her fangs into her prey, she paralyzes them," I went on.

Miss Rosonoff's back was still toward the class as she wrote on the board. The chalk made that awful squeaky noise it sometimes does.

I stopped, looked behind me for a second and noticed her hand was shaking. Then I went on. "Charlotte wraps the silk coming from her spinneret around her prey. Spider webbing is almost as strong as nylon. Here, I'll try to get her to spin some for you."

I took the screen cover off the mouth of Fido's old bowl. Then I stuck my pencil into the bowl. The class was really paying attention. Jenny Sommers' mouth hung open.

I loved it.

Ever so slowly, Charlotte climbed onto my pencil. I lifted the pencil high into the air and gently shook Charlotte off.

Miss Rosonoff picked that second to turn around and check out my pet. I don't know how it happened, but somehow Charlotte landed on Miss Rosonoff's bare arm.

Miss Rosonoff managed not to scream but the girls at the front did for her. A funny noise came from deep in Miss Rosonoff's throat: "Oughkkk."

In a flash she shook Charlotte onto the floor and stomped on her. Miss Rosonoff twisted her foot back and forth.

I dropped the fish bowl and it shattered. CRASH!

"Neil," Miss Rosonoff said in a high funny voice, "You get a broom and clean that up."

For a second or two I just stared at her. There was no sound in the classroom except my breathing. Then I blinked.

"No way," I said quietly. "Clean it up yourself."

Chapter 9

CRASH!

I tore off as fast as I could so Miss Rosonoff couldn't catch me. I ran to the end of the hall and out of the building. I ran and ran and ran.

Then I had to stop for a few seconds to catch my breath. How could everything have gone so wrong? I wondered. I started running again till I got to the shortcut home through the park.

I stopped again.

Opa was there. I called to him but he didn't hear me. He was pushing Tara on a baby swing.

High, high, higher. Then he ducked under the swing.

"Opa, Opa," I called out.

He still didn't hear me. Tara was giggling and yelling. "Again Opa. Again, again, again!"

Opa laughed too. He ran around, pushed her and ducked underneath again.

"So ignore me," I muttered under my breath.

I found a can and kicked it ahead of me as I walked along, thinking about my rotten day.

I didn't know Opa took Tara to the park when I went to school. KICK.

I can't remember the last time Opa gave me an underdog. KICK.

How dare Miss Rosonoff kill Charlotte! KICK.

Why does Dad want to call that wrinkly baby Jean-Pierre? KICK.

After about a hundred more kicks, I was home. I stopped outside the house.

The Firebird gleamed in the driveway. I put my hand on the hood. It felt warm from the sun, like something alive. The driver's side was unlocked so I opened the door and slid into the pilot's seat.

My Firebird. Well, soon, anyway.

Its sleek black nose pointed towards the road.

I fiddled with the seat and got it to slide forward so I could reach the pedals. That was better. I put my hands on the steering wheel and felt strong and powerful. Hmm.

It felt good, but something was missing without the noise.

"Vrooom," I growled, but it wasn't the same.

I wondered if it would be hard to start a car. I'd seen adults do it a million times. It would be easy — and no one would mind. I got out and opened the garage door.

There on the pegboard was the key to the Firebird. *My* Firebird when Opa won the RV. I didn't look at the corner Charlotte came from, I just snatched the key from the peg.

It felt icy in my hand. I quickly pulled down the garage door and dashed back to the Firebird before my heart pounded through my chest.

Into the slot, twist the key. The Firebird started. But I wanted to hear the big sound. I touched a pedal with my foot.

VROOOM!

Yes! It sounded great.

I put one hand on the wheel and the other on the stick shift. It was easier than I thought. I could even take it down to the end of the block and back, just like the go-kart.

Nobody was around. Nobody would mind.

Very slowly I pulled the stick shift into Drive. The Firebird rolled forward.

Then I saw it. Blue and white — Dad's police car heading for home. I could still get out of this if I hurried.

I slammed my foot to the brake pedal. Or so I thought.

Suddenly the Firebird was flying.

The gas pedal, I'd hit the gas pedal!

Across the road already, I slammed down the other pedal. Too late.

CRUNCH, CRUNCH. The Firebird bumped over the curb, scraping its bottom. Now it was half on the curb, half on the grass, rolling toward the school crossing sign.

Would it stop in time?

CLUNK.

No. The engine died. The Firebird stopped. The school crossing sign snapped and clattered onto the hood. I put my head down on the steering wheel and cried.

The door flung open and Dad lifted me out, running for a few feet before he put me down.

"Are you all right?" Dad asked me in French.

I nodded. That's when he started acting really weird. First he hugged me, then he slapped a pair of handcuffs on my wrists.

What was he saying now? Why was he still talking in French to me?

He was telling me I had a right to remain silent.

And that's just what I did.

Chapter 10

Big Trouble

Dad put me in the back of the patrol car and dashed back to the Firebird. Opa came running from the park with a look of panic on his face and Tara in tow. He threw up his hands when he saw the car. Dad stopped him and they talked. Then Dad sent Tara inside.

Claude, Dad's partner, typed some stuff into the terminal in the front of the police car.

"Tow truck's on the way," he shouted out the window to Dad.

I looked over at the Firebird.

Crumpled in the front, dented on the side and

leaking something from the bottom — what had I done to that beautiful car?

Opa looked over at me then. Tears were running down his face. I'd never seen a grown-up cry before. I slid down in the seat so that I couldn't see him.

Kids started coming home from school. It was 3:30.

If I could make it 3:00 again, I'd stay in class this time. I'd sweep up the glass of Fido's bowl and scrape the black squish that was Charlotte off the floor. No problem.

If only I could be one of those kids walking home from school now. They peeked in the cruiser to see the criminal in the back — me. I slunk down lower.

After the longest wait of my life, I saw the flashing yellow lights of the tow truck. I sat up and watched.

Dad reached in the Firebird, flicked on the hazard flasher and took out the keys. Then he handed them to the tow truck driver. The driver hooked up the car and dragged it away.

I couldn't believe how many things were dangling from the bottom. How could I have done something so stupid? What was I going to say to everyone? I couldn't stay quiet for ever.

I looked around. Opa had disappeared.

Dad came back to the cruiser. He opened the back door.

"Get out," he told me. He grabbed me by the elbow as I did. He guided me all the way into the house and upstairs to my room. Then he took off my handcuffs.

"Stay there till I get back," he said, "And don't move!"

Chapter 11

Sorry, Sorry, Sorry

Suddenly I had to go to the bathroom. I didn't dare, though, even after Dad was gone.

I felt alone — really alone. Where was Tara? Where was Opa?

There was a knock at my door.

"Opa?" I called out.

"No, it's me, Omi." My grandmother came in carrying a tray with my after-school snack.

"Where's Opa? He hates me, doesn't he? He's never going to forgive me," I said to her.

Omi hugged me. "He went for a walk to have a cigarette."

"Opa quit smoking," I said.

"He's very upset, Neil. He borrowed one from Claude," she said. "He was so afraid you had been hurt. Have some hot chocolate."

I felt cold inside, and the hot chocolate warmed me.

"Your teacher called. She wanted to speak to you but she will call back," Omi said.

"Where's Tara? Is she mad at me too?" I asked.

"Oh, she wanted to try out the crib and she fell asleep." Omi smiled at me, but in a sad way. "Tara wants to stay the baby of the family. She's finding the idea of a new little one hard to accept."

"So I've noticed," I said.

"Don't worry, you'll all adjust soon. You won't remember what it was like without your little brother around." Omi patted my shoulder. "Your mom is coming home tomorrow."

"Great!" I said.

"The birth announcement was in the paper today," she told me, taking a piece of newspaper from her pocket.

I looked at it. Everybody's name was mentioned in it. Mom's, Dad's, mine, Tara's, even Omi's and Opa's. There was only one thing missing.

"Why didn't they put the baby's name in the announcement?" I asked.

"Oh, they don't know what they want to call him yet," Omi said.

"I thought they were going to call him Jean-Pierre," I said.

"No, no, your mom told me this afternoon that they still don't have a name," Omi said.

The no-name baby, I thought. Poor kid. But I felt a sneaky bit happy about it, too.

We heard the garage door open then. Omi took my cup and the plate and left quickly.

I heard Dad's footsteps, slow and sure up the stairs. Closer and closer to my room. I wanted him to yell at me. I wanted to have it over with. But I was afraid.

The door banged open.

"How could you, Neil," my father said.

I looked down at my feet.

"How could you just take your grandfather's car like that?" he asked.

"I like Opa's car," I said.

"What!" Dad hollered.

"I never meant to wreck it," I said quickly. "I just wanted to try it out, and then . . ."

"But you're too young to drive," Dad said, "and you can't just take someone's car — that's stealing."

"No! I wasn't stealing, Opa told me he was giving me the Firebird," I explained.

"Giving you the Firebird? Why would he do a thing like that?"

"Well, he's going to win an RV. The camera store has this contest. He said when he won it he'd give me the Firebird," I told Dad.

"When he won it," Dad repeated like I was crazy. "Why does he think he's winning it?"

"I guess he doesn't. But I entered the whole pad of entry forms for him at the camera shop. How can he not win?" I wondered.

Dad sighed. "Because, Neil, that was

probably the third pad of forms put out by that store alone. Not to mention every other camera store across Canada."

"Oh, I didn't think," I mumbled.

"That's what this is all about, isn't it? You not thinking before doing something," Dad scolded.

I looked Dad in the eye now. "I'm sorry, Dad. I'm really sorry about the Firebird."

"The Firebird!" he grumbled.

"And the school crossing sign," I added quickly.

"The Firebird can be fixed. The school crossing sign, too," Dad yelled. "What if you'd been hurt? What if Opa and Tara had walked home five minutes earlier?"

I might have hit them, I realized. Suddenly, I felt cold again.

"Neil?" Dad said.

I couldn't think of a sorry big enough to cover this one.

The telephone rang then. Dad went to answer it.

After a few minutes, he called me. "Neil, it's for you. Miss Rosonoff."

Oh no! Worse and worse trouble! She would have told him how I'd talked back to her and run off.

I didn't dare look at Dad as he handed me the phone.

"Hello?"

"Neil, I'm so sorry about killing your spider today. It just startled me so much, the spider landing on me like that. I've always been afraid of them," she apologized.

"That's O.K.," I said.

"No, it isn't. I spoiled your demonstration. I read your project and you did such a fine job on it. Do you think you could catch another spider and maybe try again on Monday?"

"No. I don't want to bring another spider." I wanted to show something to the class though. I wanted them to think I was special in a good way for a change.

"Neil?" Miss Rosonoff said.

"Yes, Miss Rosonoff. Could I bring something, uh, somebody else though?" I suddenly remembered Omi's idea.

Miss Rosonoff was bound to like this idea a whole lot more than a spider. I told her about it.

"Of course, Neil," Miss Rosonoff said. "As long as it's all right with your parents."

I got off the phone then and faced Dad.

"You took a spider in for your Project Pet?" Dad asked me. "You and Marc cooked this up to scare the teacher, didn't you?"

"No, honest. Marc wanted to scare Miss Rosonoff with Slinky. But I'd just finished reading *Charlotte's Web* and I didn't have any other pet to show."

Dad sighed. "The teacher told me that you'd put a great deal of effort into your project."

"I did, Dad. Even on the first one about Fido," I said.

"But I can't get you a dog after you just smashed Opa's car," Dad warned.

"No, I know. I didn't change the water in the fishbowl when you told me to, either," I told him. "If I had, Fido might not have died, and maybe none of this would have happened."

"Aha, you're learning, Neil. Now, how are you going to work off the damage?" Dad asked.

"I'm too young to get a job," I said. "What if I babysit Tara for Mom, after school that is."

"That would be a big help. Let's say two hours a day until the summer holidays and we'll call it even," Dad said.

All the way till the summer. What would Marc say?

"I won't remind you about this deal. But if you keep your end of the bargain, and if you keep up the good work at school — summer seems like a good time to get a dog."

"All right!" I shouted. Even Marc would like this deal.

Now there was only one person left for me to square things away with.

Chapter 12

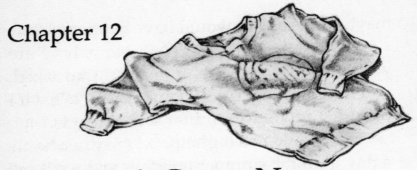

Jello-Neck Gets a Name

The next day was Saturday. Dad asked me to come with him to pick up Mom and the baby from the hospital.

I also helped him choose the baby's going home outfit. We settled on a little white sleeper with a hood and a Montreal Canadiens Hockey crest on the front.

"Ha, you used to wear this," Dad held up the sleeper. "First thing I ever bought you. Oh, that reminds me," Dad reached into his pocket and whipped out a couple of hockey cards, "Claude went through another box of Superstars."

I looked at the pictures. One was Wayne Gretzky.

"Great! Tell him thanks, I've been dying to get this one." I shoved the other cards into my shirt pocket as we headed for the hospital. But I kept the Gretzky card out and kept looking at it all the way there. Then I shoved it in my pocket with the rest.

Mom was dressed when we got there. She hugged me really tight and then let go. "Oh Neil, promise me you'll never drive another car till you're eighteen," she asked.

"I promise," I told her.

A nurse rolled my brother's fish-tank-on-wheels into the room. She checked Mom's hospital bracelet against my baby brother's. "Baby Muller-Boisvert to go home today?" she asked.

"That's right," Dad said.

"Still no name for him, eh?" She turned to my mother who shrugged her shoulders and shook her head. "This what he's wearing home?" the nurse asked as she took the Montreal Canadiens sleeper out of my hands.

"Yes," I answered.

I watched her dress the baby. Boy, was she rough! She pulled and pushed his tiny arms into the sleeper like he was made out of rubber.

"I thought you were calling him Jean-Pierre," I said suddenly.

"Jean-Pierre, ha, ha. Your dad put you up to that one," Mom said. "I hate hyphenated names. When Tara was born, your dad kept calling her Jeanette-Pierrette just to tease me. You probably wouldn't remember."

"We want a nice short name," Dad said. "Something that will look good on a hockey sweater — nothing like Thomas or William that people will change into Tommy or Billy, you know what I mean?"

Another nurse brought a wheelchair for my mother. Then the baby nurse handed the fully dressed no-name baby to her.

Dad gathered up a bunch of plants and signalled for me to get her small suitcase.

As I bent over to pick it up, my hockey cards

fell out of my shirt pocket. Wayne Gretzky stared up at me from the floor. I scooped the cards up.

"Wayne," I said out loud. "What about Wayne Boisvert?" I suggested to my mother and father.

Dad and Mom looked at each other.

"Wayne Boisvert," my mother repeated.

"Wayne Boisvert," my father repeated.

They both smiled and nodded.

Suddenly the little no-name baby was a real person — Wayne Boisvert — my little brother.

Chapter 13

The Galaxy Glows Again

"So, did Miss Rosonoff call your parents and are you in major trouble or what?" Marc asked me. He'd shown up on Sunday and I'd snuck him up to my room quickly. Nobody had actually said I was grounded anyway.

"No, Miss Rosonoff was great. She called and apologized. I can even show a new project. But I am in trouble for smashing up the Firebird." I filled Marc in on all the depressing details.

He told me he had let Slinky go.

"No kidding, how come?" I said, really surprised.

"He wouldn't eat anything. Not insects or raw meat. Not even minnows like it said in my snake book," Marc told me.

"It's a good thing you let him go," I said. "You did get to show him at school." I thought about Fido again. "And you didn't kill him."

Tara started hammering on the door then.

"Do you have to babysit today, too?" Marc asked.

"I'd better if I want to get into everyone's good books again," I said as I let Tara in. "Let's all play cards."

"Does she know how? What kind of cards are those?" Marc asked. He was looking at the eight crazy patched-up hockey cards that used to belong to him.

"Toronto Makebelieves," Tara answered.

"Hey, those are some of my traders. What happened to them?" Marc asked.

"Here," I said, flipping him my Wayne Gretzky card, "this should cover it."

"Yes! Wayne Gretzky!"

FWUMP, FWUMP, FWUMP, the cards went. And Tara won more than eight cards back. Marc wasn't in the best mood when he left for home.

That night, when we went to bed, I heard Tara's soft breathing as I read. I suddenly couldn't remember what it was like before she was around. It was even hard to remember when I didn't share my room with her.

In the middle of the night, Wayne cried. Mom got up to look after him, but Tara woke up and cried out for Mom too.

Mom didn't hear her. She was busy feeding Wayne, anyway.

"Come on, Tara, Wayne's only crying because he's a baby," I said to her. "That's the only way babies know how to talk to us."

Tara climbed out of her bed and into mine. She snuggled up to me and made me think of Wilbur the pig again. I stared up at the ceiling as Tara cried.

"Hey Tara, you're a big girl now." I said after a few moments. "Too big to sleep with the light on. Do you want to pretend you're sleeping outside under an open sky?"

She looked at me with big eyes and nodded.

"O.K. So we'll shut the door and we won't see the hall light. There." Like magic the moon, the stars and Halley's comet appeared all lit up on the ceiling.

Tara sighed and stared. I sighed too.

And that's the way we slept in our room from that night on.

Chapter 14

Project Baby

The weekend was over and Opa still wasn't talking to me much — or to anyone else for that matter. He still seemed dazed.

It was almost time to go to school, to show my new project. Everyone was going to be so impressed.

But suddenly Mom was trying to back out. "Neil, I'm sorry. I was up all night with the baby. I just can't come with you to school this morning," Mom told me.

"I'll take them," Opa said. I looked over in surprise.

"Are you sure you can manage?" Mom asked.

"Yes. It's only for a short time," Opa answered.

"Please, Mom," I begged.

"All right. Go ahead," Mom said.

"I'll push the carriage," I told them.

We left then. Opa said nothing for a while. Then he cleared his throat.

"We'll be leaving Friday," he told me as we walked.

"Don't go," I pleaded. "I'm sorry I wrecked the Firebird."

"You knew we had to go home sometime," Opa said. He looked tired.

"Opa, I'm sorry. Really sorry," I told him again.

"Your father said I set a bad example for you — speeding, breaking rules." He sighed.

"Dad's wrong. It was all my fault," I told him. "It's just that I felt like such a nobody lately. You know, the new baby, and Fido dying . . . Then when Miss Rosonoff killed Charlotte and ruined my Project Pet, I went crazy . . . and I saw you with Tara and I needed you . . . "

"You were in the park! Why didn't you call me?" Opa asked.

"I did but you didn't hear me," I said.

"Your Omi says I need a hearing aid," Opa said.

"You always make me feel like I'm important. Anyhow I sat in the Firebird and got that same feeling."

"A fancy sports car can make you forget things," Opa said. "But only for a while."

"I really thought you'd win the RV. I filled out a whole pad of entry forms and you've always been so lucky. Then you were going to give me the Firebird, remember?"

"That is what I said," Opa agreed. "But it was a stupid thing to say."

"I would never steal a car," I told him.

"I know that, Neil," Opa said. "But when I saw how wrecked the Firebird was and I realized how close you came to hurting yourself, I cried."

"I thought you were crying over the

Firebird," I told him.

"That is very sad too . . . " Opa smiled then. "But the garage can fix the car."

Exactly what Dad had said.

Opa helped me get the baby carriage over the curb on to the street. We crossed over to the schoolyard then.

Miss Rosonoff was on outdoor duty and she rushed over.

"Oh, isn't he cute," she said, peeking into the carriage. I looked at his scrunched-up face. Grown-ups are weird, I thought.

"Why don't you take him right into the classroom," she told us.

Opa and I went in.

When the bell rang, and the kids came in, Wayne woke up.

"Can I hold him? I whispered to Opa.

"Do you think that's a good idea?" Opa whispered back. "If he starts crying, we're in big trouble."

"I just have to," I told him.

Together we bent over and reached into the

carriage. Opa helped me get Wayne out. Then I sat down in Miss Rosonoff's chair and held the baby.

Wayne made these incredible baby faces, yawning, wrinkling up his nose, even smiling. Everyone laughed and was amazed.

Then I looked at his tiny bunched-up fists and I just had to touch one. Soft, soft. I couldn't believe it! Instead of throwing me a karate chop, he squeezed his fingers around mine.

That felt good. He smiled again. Dad told me that's only supposed to mean he has gas. But I felt big and important then. And nobody — not even Marc — had a pet at home that compared with a baby brother.

I started talking to the class.

"This is Wayne, my new baby brother. He's eleven days old and I named him myself."

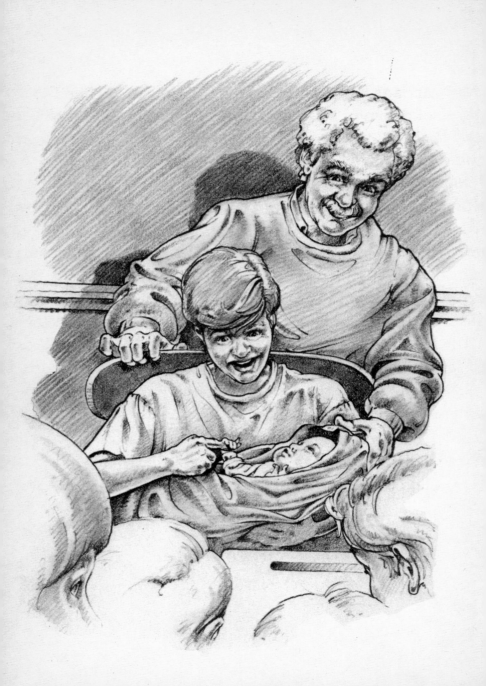